**Dedicated to
Ryan, Jeremy, Nathan
and all of the athletes at Elite Camps.**

Text & illustration copyright © 2024 by Stephanie Rudnick. All rights reserved.
Girl Baller by Stephanie Rudnick.
Published by Sport Lessons Press
www.elitecamps.com

No part of this publication may be reproduced in whole or in part, or stored in
a retrieval system, or transmitted in any form or by any means, electronic,
mechanical, photocopying, recording, or otherwise, without written permission
of the publisher/ author.
For information regarding permission, write to steph@elitecamps.com

ISBN: 978-0-9958984-2-4

In the sunny town of Hoopville lived a girl named Girl Baller, who adored basketball.

She spent hours on her driveway practicing her shot.

She loved the swish sound the net made every time she scored a basket.

One sunny day, Girl Baller was dribbling her ball near the park and saw some boys playing basketball.

With a big smile, she asked, "Can I play?"

But they shook their heads,

"Sorry, basketball is not for girls."

This made Girl Baller very sad.

But Girl Baller didn't let sadness stop her.

Instead, she thought,

"I'll show them that girls can play too!"

She decided to try out for the school basketball team.

Every day after school, you could see her practicing dribbling and shooting hoops alone in the schoolyard.

One afternoon, Coach Swish spotted

Girl Baller practicing alone.

"Are you trying out for the team?" he asked.

Girl Baller looked at her friends playing nearby

and whispered,

"They say girls can't play basketball,

but I'm going to prove them wrong.

Yes, I'll try out!"

Coach Swish said,

"Remember, the important thing is how you dribble, shoot, and hustle.

If you've got the skills, you've got a chance, just like everyone else!"

Girl Baller put up a big calendar in her bedroom.

She marked the tryout day in bright red and planned her practice schedule.

Every day, she had a new basketball challenge for herself.

She practiced early in the morning,

even before school started,

always at the schoolyard, dribbling

and shooting.

While her friends met up for playdates on weekends, Girl Baller stayed home, practicing for hours in her driveway, perfecting her shot and working on her dribbling.

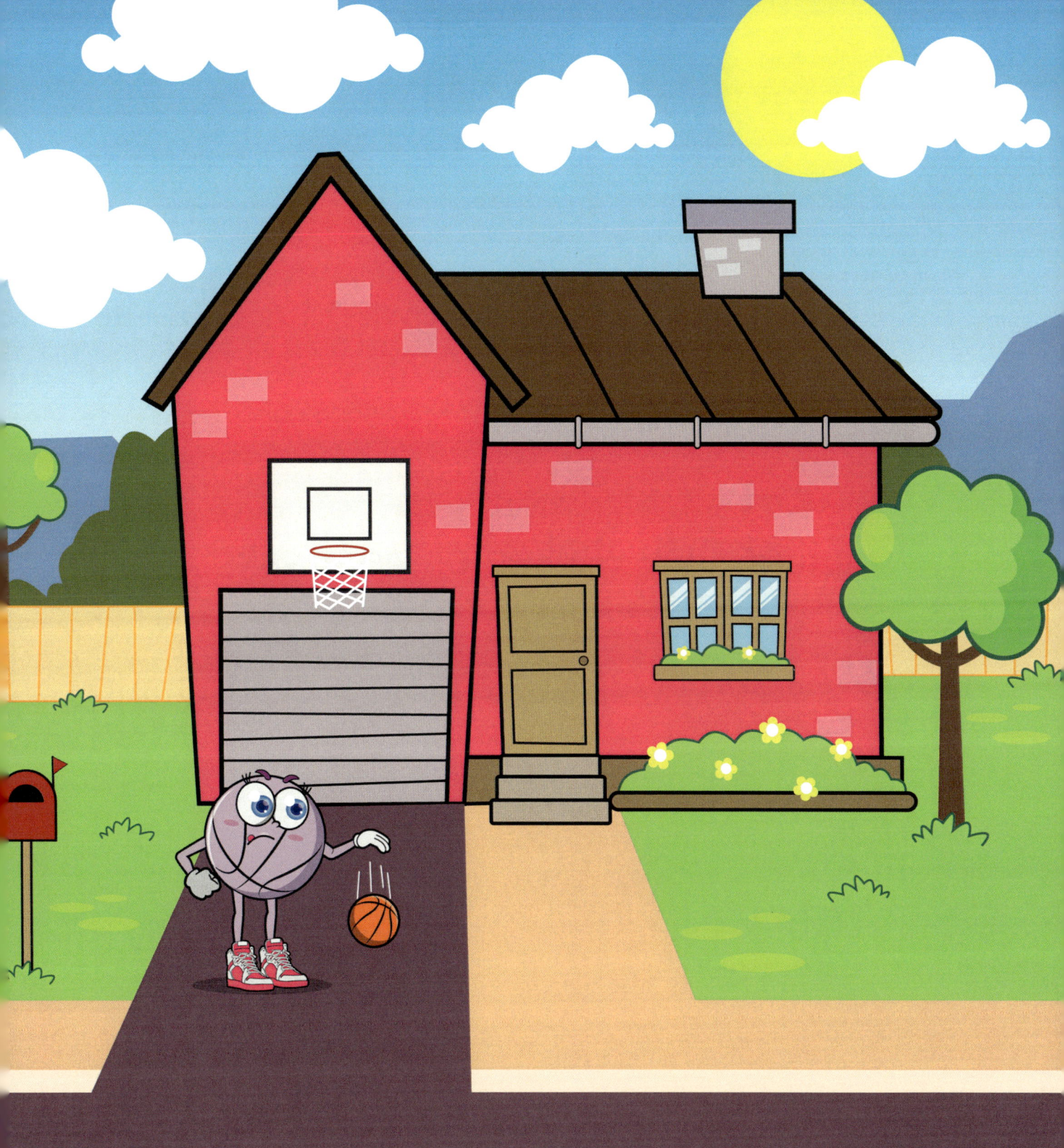

She even asked Coach Swish for extra help after school.

Together, they worked on her basketball moves and layups, practicing until the sun went down.

The tryout day arrived, and Girl Baller woke up feeling a mix of nerves and excitement.

She had butterflies dancing in her tummy.

Walking into the gym, some players looked surprised, and a few giggled.

But Girl Baller just focused, tying her shoelaces tight, ready to play her best.

When the tryout began, all giggles and whispers stopped.

Girl Baller was a whirlwind on the court, dribbling past everyone, scoring basket after basket.

She was the best player on the court!!

After the tryout,

Coach Swish gave Girl Baller a big high five.

"Your hard work really paid off. You're more skilled than anyone else who tried out today".

Girl Baller not only made the team, but the boys realized she was the best player. The boys, once doubtful, now admired her skills and even voted her as the team captain!

Girl Baller showed everyone that with practice and determination, girls can play basketball just as brilliantly as boys, maybe even better!

Questions To Ask Your Child After Reading The Book

How did Girl Baller feel when her friends said, "Sorry, basketball is not for girls"? How would you feel in that situation?

What did Girl Baller do to prove her friends wrong? How can you apply her determination in your own life?

Why do you think Coach Swish told Girl Baller that all that matters is dribbling, shooting, and hustling on the court?

How did Girl Baller prepare for the tryout? What are some things you can do to prepare for something important to you?

How do you think Girl Baller felt when Coach Swish said she was more skilled than all the other ballers?

About The Author

Stephanie Rudnick is a mother, a writer, a motivational speaker, and the founding owner of Elite Camps, one of the largest basketball organizations of its kind in Canada.

Stephanie's passion for basketball is stronger than ever.

Once a high-level player, she now helps athletes develop their on-court skills while ensuring that they, their parents, and their coaches all understand how the lessons learned on-court can prepare them for success in life.

Stephanie lives in Ontario with her husband, David, and their three sons.

www.elitecamps.com

A Word By The Author

If you enjoyed this book, it would be wonderful if you could take a moment to leave a lovely review on Amazon, as your kind feedback is very appreciated and so very important to help spread the word about books designed to support families on their sports journey. Thank you so very much for your time.

Click this link to leave a review
https://linktr.ee/stephanierudnick

THANK YOU..

Made in the USA
Las Vegas, NV
27 March 2025